Postman Pat
and the Spring Cleaning Day

Story by **John Cunliffe**
Pictures by **Joan Hickson**

From the original Television designs by Ivor Wood

GUILD PUBLISHING LONDON

This edition published 1989 by
Guild Publishing
By arrangement with André Deutsch Limited

Text copyright © 1988 by John Cunliffe
Illustrations copyright © 1988 by André Deutsch Limited
Scholastic Publications Limited and
Woodland Animations Limited
All rights reserved

CN 5268

Made and printed in Belgium by Proost

It was spring in Greendale, and
everyone was busy. They were spring-
cleaning. Everywhere that Pat went
there was a brushing, and a beating,
and a sweeping, and a polishing, and
a washing, and a vacuuming going on.
Carpets were hung out in the sun.

Pots and pans shone like new. Chairs stood on tables. It was awful! There was nowhere to sit, and the dust made Pat sneeze.

"I'll be glad when it's all done," said Pat.

When he called at Thompson Ground,
Mrs. Thompson was polishing the
fireplace. It had brass knobs and
fittings all over it, and she rubbed at
them till they shone like lamps.

"You want to be careful, with all that rubbing," said Pat, "you'll have a genie jumping out, like that one in Aladdin."

"I wish it would," said Mrs. Thompson. "It could help me with my spring cleaning."

"Do you think you could give Jess a rub, while you're at it?" said Pat, laughing. Jess went and hid behind the dresser. He thought he would do his own cleaning. A good lick, and a rub with his paw, would be good enough for him.

"It's the first time it's been warm enough to let the fire out," said Mrs. Thompson. "I do like to give it a good polish. It looks more welcoming. Have a cup of tea, Pat. The kettle's boiled. Help yourself."

Pat went into the kitchen to brew the tea. Mrs. Thompson went outside to shake the rug.

Jess came out, and sniffed at the cold fireplace. It was a big old fireplace. Jess could see the chimney going up into the darkness. He seemed to like it. He put his head on one side. He listened. He listened to something; a very small sound, far, far away. His whiskers twitched. His tail went up like a car aerial.

"Tea up!" called Pat, coming back with the tray.

"Grand!" said Mrs. Thompson, coming back with the rug. "Would Jess like some milk?"

"Come and have some milk, Jess," said Pat, looking behind the dresser. "He's not here! Jess! Where are you? Come on, Jess."

"He was here a minute ago," said Mrs. Thompson.

"I expect he's gone to see if there are any mice in your barn," said Pat. "Let's get this tea while it's still hot," said Mrs. Thompson.

They had a good drink and a good chat. Pat told Mrs. Thompson all the Greendale news.

"The Pottages have bought a new three-piece suite. And Mrs. Goggins is having a new cooker put in, this morning. Ted's mended Granny Dryden's clock, and Miss Hubbard has opened last year's rhubarb wine.

And Dr. Gilbertson has a new car, a silver Sierra. Oh, yes, and Peter Fogg's crashed into a tree on his motorbike, but he's not badly hurt. And the Reverend Timms is going to Australia for a holiday and to see his sister."

"There's always something going on in Greendale," said Mrs. Thompson.

"Did you hear anything, Pat?"

"What about?"

"No, I mean just now. While you were talking. A noise."

"What sort of noise?" said Pat.

"A scratchy sort of noise. There it is again. Listen!"

"It's coming from the fireplace," said Pat.

"It's up the chimney," said Mrs. Thompson.

"You haven't got mice up your chimney, have you?" said Pat.

"I hope not," said Mrs. Thompson. "I do hope not. There are so many nooks

and crannies in this old house, that . . . oh, goodness me! Look, Pat!" What had made Mrs. Thompson shout, and almost drop her tea?

A black shape, too big for a mouse, came scrabbling down the chimney, jumped out of the fireplace, and ran for the door.

"What was that?" shouted Pat.

Whatever it was, it had left a trail of sooty paw-marks across the clean rug, and across the polished floor.

They chased after it, outside and across the yard. Then they saw it! It was a huge black cat, spitting and showing its claws, and sending the hens running in all directions.

"Don't go near it," Pat shouted. "It looks dangerous to me."

Then Towser, the dog, came out of his
kennel like a growling rocket, and
chased the strange black cat all round
the yard. The black cat jumped for the
wall, slipped, and fell in the water-
trough. Oh, what a splashing and a
noise there was!

There was the strange cat swimming for its life, with Towser jumping about and barking his head off.

But when the black cat crawled out of the water and shook itself, it was not a black cat any more. It was a black-and-white cat.

"I know that cat," said Mrs. Thompson. "I've seen it somewhere. Come here, Towser, leave it alone. It won't hurt you. It's only a cat."

"It's Jess!" said Pat. "Jess, what have you been doing? Come on, puss. See, it is Jess. He was covered in soot, and the water washed it off. Poor Jess."

Pat picked Jess up and gave him a cuddle. He was shivering with cold and fright, but he soon felt better.

"I do believe your Jess went up my chimney, looking for mice," said Mrs. Thompson. "Did you, Jess? Is that what you did, you naughty cat? And just look at my nice clean floor. See what a mess you've made."

Jess couldn't tell Mrs. Thompson what he'd been up to, and he couldn't say he was sorry, but he did *look* very sorry. "Never mind, Jess," said Mrs. Thompson, "we'll not be cross with you. But we cannot have you making sooty paw-marks in all the kitchens of Greendale. Keep hold of him, Pat. I won't be a minute."

Mrs. Thompson went into the kitchen again, and came back with a plastic bowl full of soapy water.

"Just pop him in," she said, "and we'll spring-clean him in no time."

"But Jess doesn't like . . ." Pat began.
But he was too late.

Jess was in the water, and fighting to
get out again.

It was no good! Mrs. Thompson was used to all kinds of cats. She held Jess firmly, until he was clean all over. Then she rinsed him under the tap, to get all the soap out, popped him in a

big old towel, and wrapped him up in
it until he was dry.

When Pat unwrapped Jess from the towel, it was a new cat that stepped out. His fur was clean and fluffy, and he smelled like a flower. But he looked cross. Very cross.

"Poor Jess," Pat laughed. "He doesn't like baths; but he hasn't looked so beautiful in years."

"You'll have to put him in for the Reverend's pet show in September," said Mrs. Thompson.

"I might do that," said Pat. "I might well."

"And I hope that will teach him not to go up chimneys and mess clean floors up," said Mrs. Thompson.

"Let me give you a hand," said Pat,
"to clean it up."

"Oh, it's all right, really. You'd best be
on your way with all those letters,"
said Mrs. Thompson, smiling. "I'll
soon get straight. I've seen worse
messes than that."

But Pat helped, all the same.

Soon, it was time to go. Pat was on his
way, with a, "Cheerio, Mrs.
Thompson!" and "Thanks for the
tea."
"I wonder, Jess, if you could win a
prize at the pet show?" said Pat, as
they went along the road. "I wonder.
It's a good idea, that."

Jess had his own thoughts about baths and pet shows, but he wasn't telling anyone what they were. One thing is sure; he never went up a chimney again.